D0819629

T1-AYP-185

NATURAL WONDERS

Uluru

Sacred Rock of the Australian Desert

Jennifer Hurtig

W

WEIGL PUBLISHERS INC.

2635 Homestead Road
Santa Clara, CA 95051

Published by Weigl Publishers Inc.
350 5th Avenue, Suite 3304, PMB 6G
New York, NY 10118-0069

Website: www.weigl.com

Copyright ©2007 WEIGL PUBLISHERS INC.
All rights reserved. No part of this publication may be reproduced, stored in a retrieval system, or transmitted in any form or by any means, electronic, mechanical, photocopying, recording, or otherwise, without the prior written permission of the publisher.

Library of Congress Cataloging-in-Publication Data

Hurtig, Jennifer.
  Uluru / Jennifer Hurtig.
      p. cm. -- (Natural wonders)
  Includes bibliographical references and index.
  ISBN 1-59036-448-1 (library binding : alk. paper) -- ISBN 1-59036-454-6 (soft cover : alk. paper)
  1. Ayers Rock (N.T.)--Juvenile literature. 2. Uluru-Kata Tjuta National Park (N.T.)--Juvenile literature. I. Title. II. Series:
Natural wonders (Weigl Publishers)
  DU398.A9H87 2007
  994.29'1--dc22
                              2006016147

Printed in the United States of America
1 2 3 4 5 6 7 8 9 0 08 07 06 05 04

Editor
Heather C. Hudak

Design
Terry Paulhus

Photograph Credits

Every reasonable effort has been made to trace ownership and to obtain permission to reprint copyright material. The publishers would be pleased to have any errors or omissions brought to their attention so that they may be corrected in subsequent printings.

Cover: Uluru is made from a type of rock called arkose, a sandstone that contains the minerals quartz and feldspar. Arkose appears as different colors, depending on the Sun's position in the sky.

All of the Internet URLs given in the book were valid at the time of publication. However, due to the dynamic nature of the Internet, some addresses may have changed, or sites may have ceased to exist since publication. While the author and publisher regret any inconvenience this may cause readers, no responsibility for any such changes can be accepted by either the author or the publisher.

Contents

Rising above the Plains 4

Where in the World? 6

A Trip Back in Time 8

Geology at Work 10

Wildlife around Uluru 12

Early Explorers 14

The Big Picture 16

People of Uluru 18

Cultural Heritage 20

Natural Attractions 22

Key Issues: Climbing Uluru 24

Timeline 26

What Have You Learned? 28

Find Out for Yourself 30

Glossary/Index 32

Rising above the Plains

Uluru is a monolith, or massive rock formation, that rises high above the plains of central Australia. It is composed of a single piece of **sandstone** rock. From far away, Uluru looks very smooth, but close up, it has many holes, caves, ribs, and valleys.

Nearby lies another rock formation, Kata Tjuta. Together, Uluru and Kata Tjuta form a national park. This park is protected as a **UNESCO World Heritage Site** because it has a strong cultural and historical value. People come to see the interesting rock formations at Uluru-Kata Tjuta and to learn about the culture of Australia's Aboriginal people. **Aboriginal Australians** have lived at Uluru for more than 30,000 years.

Uluru rises 1,143 feet (348 meters) above sea level.

Uluru-Kata Tjuta National Park Facts

- Uluru-Kata Tjuta National Park has been named a World Heritage Site for its natural and cultural values.

- Both Uluru and Kata Tjuta are important ceremonial and cultural places to many Aboriginal Australians.

- More than 150 species of birds have been recorded in the park.

- Many lizard species are found in the park, including the rare desert skink.

- Uluru is the largest single rock in the world.

- The tallest point of Kata Tjuta is called Mount Olga. It reaches a height of 1,791 feet (546 meters).

- Uluru measures almost 5.8 miles (9.4 kilometers) around the base.

- Kata Tjuta means "many heads" in the local Aboriginal language.

- Kata Tjuta is composed of 36 rock domes that lie 26 miles (42 km) west of Uluru. They are made of a mix of pebbles, boulders, and cobbles cemented together with mud and sand.

Uluru Locator

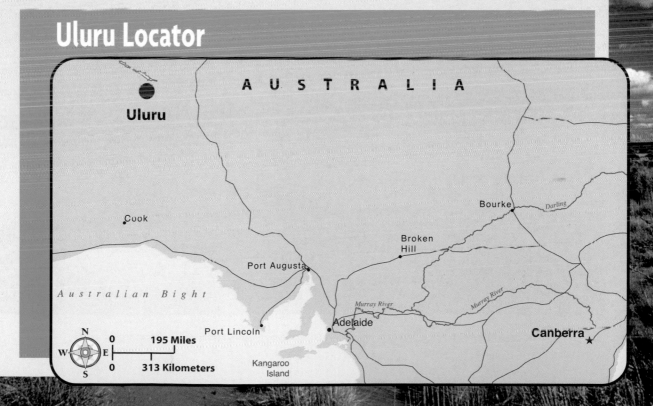

Where in the World?

Uluru-Kata Tjuta National Park is located in the southwestern area of the Northern Territory of Australia. This central area of Australia is often called the "Red Center" because the soil is so red. This area is very dry and hot and has few towns or settlements. It is a land of deserts and mountain ranges. There are mountain ranges both to the north and south of the park.

Uluru-Kata Tjuta National Park lies more than 1,000 miles (1,600 km) from any major city in Australia. The nearest large town is Alice Springs, more than 200 miles (320 km) to the northeast. Most visitors to the national park fly into Alice Springs. It is a popular winter resort for vacationers and tourists, as well as a center for mining and livestock rearing.

Uluru is made from arkose rock that is nearly 500 million years old.

Fires

Early explorers sometimes noticed that there was smoke coming from Uluru. This is because Aboriginal Australians used a *tjangi*, or fire stick, to burn patches of bushy spinifex grass. As the old plants burned, their nutrients would sink into the ground and help new plants to grow. Aboriginal Australians burned spinifex grass to encourage new growth of grasses that would attract animals, such as kangaroos, which they hunted for food.

Controlled fires are still lit today, mostly in winter. This helps to burn off dry grasses that could become fuel for a big fire in summer. Uncontrolled fires can do a great deal of damage. In 1976, two fires burned 76 percent of the park's plants.

After a fire has passed over an area, seeds lying in the ground can develop into new plants.

A Trip Back in Time

Aboriginal Australians still live in the area around Uluru and Kata Tjuta. An Aboriginal group called Anangu are the traditional owners of Uluru. Anangu have their own creation story about Uluru. They believe that there was nothing on Earth until their **ancestors** came. Then, the ancestral creator beings formed the landscape and rocks that can be seen today. Anangu believe that they, as well as the plants and animals that live around them, are descended from these ancestral spirits.

Anangu explanations about how Uluru developed are different from those of geologists. Geologists believe that the rock that makes up Uluru formed about 550 million years ago during the **Cambrian period**.

Aboriginal Australians gather at the Yeperenye Federation Festival to celebrate their culture through dance, art, and music.

Caves

Along the edges of Uluru and Kata Tjuta are shallow caves. These caves provided Anangu people with shelter from harsh weather. The Aboriginal Australians also held sacred ceremonies here and drew paintings on the walls of the caves.

Ikari is a cave on the southeastern side of Uluru. It contains very old animal bones and teeth. These bones are hundreds of years old. They came from animals that once lived in Uluru or were carried into the cave by other animals, such as owls.

The name of this cave comes from an Anangu story of a Willy Wagtail woman called Ikari, who once lived in the cave. A Willy Wagtail is a small bird found in Australia.

Geology at Work

During the Cambrian period, there were violent movements of Earth's **crust**. Molten, or liquid, rock reached the surface and created a range of mountains made of a hard rock called granite. Over the next 50 million years, the mountains **eroded**. This process created thick layers of **sediment** over a wide area. Earth's crust again shifted dramatically about 310 to 340 million years ago. This shifting made the layers of sediment tilt.

Today, the layers can be seen as ridges on the sides of Uluru. Weathering by wind and water have given Uluru its unique shape. Only the top of the Uluru rock is visible. Much of it lies underground. Scientists estimate that Uluru may extend 3.6 miles (5.8 km) underground.

The ridges on the sides of Uluru are the tilted layers of sandstone that were laid down millions of years ago.

The Importance of Water

There are many valleys and **gorges** in Uluru-Kata Tjuta. Rainstorms formed these gorges over millions of years. Water flowing down the rocks created large grooves where valleys are today.

Water is very important to the people who live in this desert. The average yearly rainfall in this area is less than 9 inches (23 centimeters). Rainwater is quickly absorbed into the ground.

Despite this, there usually is water around the base of Uluru. When it rains, the water runs down the rock and collects in pools. Water also can be found in the layers of sand in a valley between Uluru and Kata Tjuta. This water eventually drains into Lake Amadeus, a few miles to the north.

The Mutitjulu watering hole in Uluru-Kata Tjuta provides moisture for the desert animals.

Wildlife around Uluru

The area around Uluru is full of wildlife. More than 20 species of mammals live there. Some small mammals, such as mulgaras and moles, live in burrows and tunnels in the sand. Bats live in caves and cracks in the rocks. Larger mammals, such as red kangaroos, dingoes, and wallaroos, also live around Uluru. Camels, foxes, cats, dogs, and rabbits have been brought to Australia from other countries. They are causing great harm to the natural environment.

Reptiles, such as pythons and skinks, and amphibians, such as frogs, thrive in this region. Some bird species live near Uluru all year long, but others only arrive after there has been rain. Anangu name birds for their calls. They use the name *piyar-piyarpa* for galahs or *walawuru* for wedgetail eagles.

■ **Dingoes are wild dogs that live in packs throughout much of Australia. They hunt small mammals and birds, but can survive on plants if there is no prey available.**

Plants

Plants that grow in the Uluru area must adapt to the hot, dry conditions. The mulga is a common tree in Australia. This tree has developed a survival strategy to deal with bush fires. Its seeds require heat to crack and **germinate**.

Trees are an important resource for both people and animals. Their wood is used as firewood. Their leafy branches provide shelter for kangaroos, finch nests, and mistletoe fruit.

Shrubs, such as corkwood trees or crimson turkey bush, provide Anangu with sweet nectar. Grasses are dry and somewhat prickly. Many flowers bloom in the dry desert only after rainfall. Poisonous fruit also grow in this area. Aboriginal Australians know which fruit can be eaten.

The plants around Uluru are mainly grasses, low-growing shrubs, and stunted trees.

Early Explorers

The first humans arrived in Australia around 60,000 years ago. They were the ancestors of today's Aboriginal Australians. These people knew about Uluru for tens of thousands of years before the first European discovered the enormous rock. The first person of European descent to see Uluru was Ernest Giles in October, 1872. He saw it from far away and described it as "the remarkable pebble."

On July 19, 1873, William Gosse, a surveyor who was mapping unknown areas of Australia, arrived at Uluru and named it Ayers Rock. It was named after Sir Henry Ayers, the chief secretary of South Australia. Many tourists and miners had come to Uluru by the 1950s. The Australian government established Uluru, Kata Tjuta, and the surrounding land as a national park in 1958.

■ Explorer William Ernest Powell Giles was an experienced surveyor. He wanted to cross Australia from east to west.

Biography

William Gosse (1842–1881)

In 1873, explorer and surveyor William Christie Gosse became the first non-Aboriginal person to reach Uluru. He worked for the surveyor-general's office and had already surveyed the far northern and southeastern districts of South Australia.

After those explorations, the government sent Gosse to explore more of South Australia. Gosse was looking to find a route between Alice Springs and Perth, on Australia's southwestern coast, when he reached Uluru. He and his team of men had to turn back before they reached Perth, but they mapped more than 60,000 square miles (155,000 sq km) of previously uncharted land.

Facts of Life

Born: December 11, 1842

Hometown: Hoddesdon, Hertfordshire, England

Occupation: Explorer, Surveyor

Died: August 12, 1881

The Big Picture

A monolith is a single massive rock or stone. Uluru is just one of many monoliths located in Australia. The world's largest monolith is Australia's Mount Augustus. It is 2.5 times larger than Uluru. There are many other monoliths around the world, too. Some of these include El Capitan in the United States, Aso Rock in Nigeria, and Frau Holle Stone in Germany.

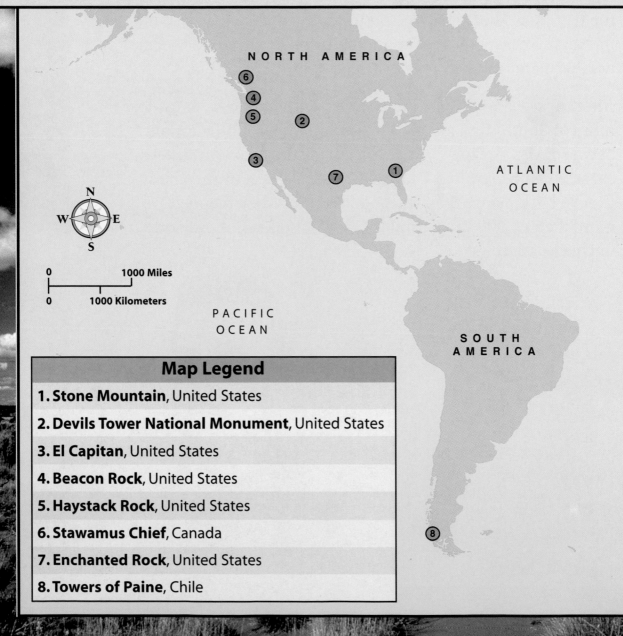

Map Legend

1. **Stone Mountain**, United States
2. **Devils Tower National Monument**, United States
3. **El Capitan**, United States
4. **Beacon Rock**, United States
5. **Haystack Rock**, United States
6. **Stawamus Chief**, Canada
7. **Enchanted Rock**, United States
8. **Towers of Paine**, Chile

ASIA

EUROPE

AFRICA

INDIAN
OCEAN

AUSTRALIA

Map Legend

9. **Frau Holle Stone**, Germany
10. **Humber Stone**, England
11. **King Arthur's Stone**, England
12. **Logan Stone**, England
13. **Odin Stone**, Scotland
14. **Rock of Gibraltar**, Gibraltar
15. **Ben Amera**, Mauritania
16. **Brandberg Mountain**, Namibia
17. **Aso Rock**, Nigeria
18. **Savandurga**, India
19. **Uluru**, Australia
20. **Mount Augustus**, Australia
21. **Mount Coolum**, Australia
22. **Mount Wudinna**, Australia

People of Uluru

At one time, Anangu people moved around to hunt and to find food. Some Anangu today still live off the land's resources. They gather wild fruits, seeds, and vegetables, and hunt animals for food, including kangaroos, lizards, and birds.

Many Anangu have combined their traditional culture with modern conveniences. About 300 Anangu live near Uluru in the community of Mutitjulu. Many work in the park alongside park rangers, sharing their knowledge of the area with the rangers and visitors. They lead tours of the site and teach people how to live in the hot, dry climate.

While visiting the Aboriginal Cultural Center in Uluru-Kata Tjuta National Park, a park ranger offered the king and queen of Sweden insect grubs and other bush food.

Anangu Beliefs

The basis of Anangu knowledge is called *Tjukurpa*. The word *Wapar* is used to describe Anangu laws and beliefs. These two words involve many concepts. They include history, the present, and the future. These words also describe the way people, plants, animals, and the land interact, as well as the knowledge of how these relationships came to be.

Tjukurpa is passed on through oral storytelling. It is not written in books. To help Anangu remember Tjukurpa, they have created songs, dances, and art. Stories often are passed on during ceremonies. Certain people maintain their own sections of Tjukurpa. Some stories are known only by women, and other stories are just for men.

■ **During ceremonies, Aboriginal Australians decorate their face and body with paint made from white clay and berries.**

Cultural Heritage

Uluru is a sacred and important site for many Aboriginal Australians. Sacred ceremonies and storytellings about ancestors take place at Uluru. Aboriginal Australians have marked the rocks with drawings, paintings, carvings, and engravings.

Many of the landscapes have meaning to Anangu. They represent creation stories and knowledge that have been passed down for generations. Anangu beliefs discourage changes to the land.

The Australian government now protects certain Aboriginal Australian sacred sites, such as Uluru. In 1993, Ayers Rock was renamed Ayers Rock/Uluru to combine both the English and traditional Aboriginal names for the rock. Then in 2002, the order of the names was reversed to Uluru/Ayers Rock.

In 1985, Uluru-Kata Tjuta National Park land was returned to the Anangu.

Puzzler

Anangu living around Uluru used art to pass on stories. They painted on cave walls and drew pictures in the sand. They also painted their bodies. Their designs told stories and had religious and ceremonial meaning. The Anangu still create works of art, but they no longer paint on the rocks.

Q Why did Anangu use artwork to tell stories?

A The Anangu created works of art to pass on stories from one generation to the next, and in this way, the stories were preserved.

Natural Attractions

Despite its remoteness, hundreds of thousands of visitors make the trip to Uluru each year. The cultural center in the park has displays and exhibits about the Anangu way of life. People also enjoy walking through the valleys. The main walking trails are the Valley of the Winds and the Olga Gorge.

Depending on the time of day, Uluru seems to be different colors. This is because ash, dust particles, and **water vapor** in the **atmosphere** filter or remove some of the blue light from the Sun's rays. This means that more red light reaches the rocks than blue light. The atmosphere is not very thick around midday, but in the mornings and evenings, the atmosphere is thicker, so the light is more filtered. At these times, the sunlight reaching the rocks is mainly from the red end of the **spectrum**.

▬ **Visitors to Uluru watch the rock change color during sunset and sunrise.**

Be Prepared

When hiking through Uluru-Kata Tjuta, you must plan what to wear and what to bring because it can be very hot or windy. The clothes you bring depend on the season of your visit.

If you are traveling in the summer months, it can be very dry and hot. Make sure you wear comfortable shoes, a hat, and sunscreen. Your clothing should be light, such as shorts and a t-shirt.

In the cooler months, it can get cold at night. From August to November, it is very windy in this area. Make sure you wear more than one layer of clothing. You may want to wear warmer clothes, such as a heavy jacket and long pants.

TIP: Make sure that you drink plenty of water so that you do not become dehydrated, or dried out. Dehydration is a huge problem in the desert.

Climbing Uluru

Many people are fascinated by Uluru and want to climb the large rock. However, Uluru is sacred to the Anangu, so they do not climb its landscape. Anangu believe that visitors should respect their rules as they are guests on Anangu land. In 1983, the prime minister of Australia, Bob Hawke, promised to ban climbing of the rock, but this did not happen.

Climbing Uluru is a popular activity. In 1976, a chain handhold was put on the rock to give people something to hold onto while climbing. The climb up Uluru is long and steep, and, almost every year, people die attempting to climb the rock. Most deaths are caused by heart attacks or heart failure.

▬ **When desert temperatures soar and high winds make the trek too dangerous, Uluru is closed to climbers.**

CLIMB CLOSED DUE TO

FORECAST TEMP. 36DEG. OR ABOVE

Anangu also do not want people to photograph the areas of Uluru where their ceremonies take place. Some areas of Uluru are only to be seen by men. Other parts of the giant rock are only to be seen by women. Anangu fear that visitors might take photographs in these areas. It would then be possible for Anangu to see pictures of forbidden places. Signs have now been put up in these places to prevent visitors from taking photographs of these sacred sites.

Should people be allowed to climb the rock?

YES	NO
As long as tourists are respectful of the land, they should be allowed to climb Uluru.	Uluru is a spiritual place for the Anangu, and tourists should not be allowed to climb the rock. There are many tours offered around the base of the rock that provide a great view of this natural wonder.
Tourists travel great distances to climb Uluru, and much money is raised through the tourism industry.	Climbers must be wary of the dangers involved in the climb. The chain used to guide people who climb the rock stops halfway to the top. Some people have fallen to their deaths making the climb.

Timeline

4–5 billion years ago
Earth forms.

550 million years ago
Land forms that is now Uluru.

310–340 million years ago
Earth's crust shifts
dramatically, and the
layers of sediment
that are now Uluru tilt.

65 million years ago
Dinosaurs become extinct.

50 million years ago
Australia separates from the
other continents.

60,000 years ago
Ancestors of Aboriginal
Australians begin living
in Australia.

30,000 years ago
Windswept sands cover the
plains surrounding Uluru.

1770
James Cook claims Australia
for Great Britain.

Uluru is a prominent feature in a
mainly flat desert landscape.

A desert death
adder lies on
warm sand in
the Alice Springs
Desert Park.

1872
Explorer Ernest Giles sees the
rock from far away.

1873
European explorer William
Gosse is the first European to
discover Uluru and explores
the surrounding area.

1958
Uluru, Kata-Tjuta, and
the surrounding area
are established as a
national park.

1976
A chain handhold is put
on Uluru.

The mulgara is a rare pouched mammal found around Uluru. It feeds on insect grubs.

Much of the landscape around Alice Springs is stony and dry.

1993
Uluru is renamed Ayers Rock/Uluru to incorporate both the English and traditional Aboriginal names for the rock.

2000
The opening ceremonies for the 2000 Summer Olympics are held at Uluru-Kata Tjuta National Park.

2002
The order of the names is reversed to Uluru/Ayers Rock.

2002
Wildfires burn much of Uluru-Kata Tjuta National Park.

2005
Rowan Foley is appointed as the first-ever indigenous park manager at Uluru-Kata Tjuta National Park.

1978–1985
Officers of Northern Territory's Parks and Wildlife Service run the park.

1985
Uluru is given back to Anangu.

1987
Uluru-Kata Tjuta National Park is designated a UNESCO World Heritage Site for its natural and cultural value.

What Have You Learned?

True or False?

Decide whether the following statements are true or false.
If the statement is false, rewrite it to make it true.

1. Uluru is a sacred place to Anangu.

2. Uluru-Kata Tjuta stays warm year round.

3. No plants grow here because fires burn them.

4. "Willy Wagtail" is a kind of rabbit.

5. Kata Tjuta means "many heads."

6. Anangu no longer use the natural resources of the land anymore.

ANSWERS

1. True

2. False. Winters are cooler with strong winds. Temperatures can fall below freezing.

3. False. Some plants rely on fire to reproduce. Other plants become resistant to fire to survive.

4. False. Willy Wagtail is the name for a small Australian bird.

5. True

6. False. Some Anangu continue to hunt for game or collect plants for food or medicine.

Short Answer

Answer the following questions using information from the book.

1. What is the name of Anangu's basis of knowledge and beliefs?

2. When did Uluru form?

3. Why did the name of Ayers Rock change to Uluru/Ayers Rock?

4. Why should people not climb Uluru?

5. Is there much water near Uluru year round?

ANSWERS
1. Tjukurpa
2. More than 550 million years ago.
3. To incorporate the Aboriginal Australian name for the rock.
4. Uluru is sacred to Aboriginal Australians.
5. No. Uluru receives little rainfall, and the ground soaks up water quickly.

Multiple Choice

Choose the best answer for the following questions.

1. What color does Uluru sometimes appear?
   a) green
   b) yellow
   c) red
   d) blue

2. Where in Australia is Uluru-Kata Tjuta National Park located?
   a) South Australia
   b) Northern Territory
   c) Queensland
   d) New South Wales

3. Which of these mammals is not native to Uluru?
   a) camel
   b) mulgara
   c) bat
   d) kangaroo

4. How many rock domes is Kata Tjuta composed of?
   a) 5
   b) 16
   c) 36
   d) 45

ANSWERS
1. c
2. b
3. a
4. c

Find Out for Yourself

Books

Arnold, Caroline. *Uluru: Australia's Aboriginal Heart.* New York: Clarion Books, 2004.

Marshall, Diana. *Aboriginal Australians.* New York: Weigl Publishers Inc., 2004.

Finlay, Carol. *Aboriginal Art of Australia: Exploring Cultural Traditions.* Lerner Publishing Group, 1999.

Websites

Use the Internet to discover more about the people, plants, animals, and geology of the Uluru-Kata Tjuta National Park.

Uluru-Kata Tjuta National Park
www.deh.gov.au/parks/uluru
This is the official site of the Australian government authority that oversees this park.

World Heritage Sites
http://whc.unesco.org/sites/447.htm
This is the official website of World Heritage Sites around the world.

Australian Tourism
www.atn.com.au/nt/south/uluru.htm
This website gives information on what to do at Uluru and provides information about the site.

Skill Matching Page

What did you learn? Look at the questions in the "Skills" column. Compare them to the page number of the answers in the "Page" column. Refresh your memory by reading the "Answer" column below.

SKILLS	ANSWER	PAGE
What facts did I learn from this book?	I learned that the rocks of Uluru-Kata Tjuta are sacred sites for Aboriginal Australians.	9, 20–21, 24–25
What skills did I learn?	I learned how to read a map.	5, 16–17
What activities did I do?	I answered the questions in the quiz.	28–29
How can I find out more about Uluru-Kata Tjuta?	I can read the books and visit the websites from the Find Out for Yourself page.	30
How can I get involved?	I can choose not to climb Uluru when I visit the park.	24–25

Glossary

Aboriginal Australians: the descendants of the earliest-known peoples in Australia
ancestors: people from whom a modern person is descended
atmosphere: the mass of air surrounding Earth
Cambrian period: a period in time between 550 million and 505 million years ago
crust: the rocky, outer layer of Earth
eroded: worn away, or ground down
germinate: to begin to grow, or sprout
gorges: narrow and deep passages that cut through rock
sandstone: a sedimentary rock formed by the compaction of sand, held together by a natural cement
sediment: sand or silt gradually deposited by wind or water and compacted to become hard
spectrum: a continuous range of colors made of different wavelengths of light
UNESCO World Heritage Site: a place that is of natural or cultural importance to the entire world. UNESCO is an abbreviation for United Nations Educational, Scientific. and Cultural Organization.
water vapor: barely visible water, suspended in the air as a gas

Index

Aboriginal Australians 4, 7, 8–9, 12, 13, 14, 18, 22, 24, 25, 27
animals 5, 11, 12, 13, 18, 26, 27

caves 9, 12
climbing 24, 25

deserts 6, 11, 13, 16, 17, 23, 26

geology 4, 5, 6, 8, 10
Giles, Ernest 14, 26
Gosse, William 14, 15, 26

Northern Territory 6

plants 7, 12, 13

water 11, 23
World Heritage Site 4, 5, 27